THE ANTARCTIC EXPRESS

Written by
KENNETH HITE

Illustrated by
CHRISTINA RODRIGUEZ

Editing & Layout by
MICHELLE NEPHEW

ATLAS GAMES

SAINT PAUL

To Cailin.

   – KH

With sincere thanks to
Greta and Emmet. The
penguins are for Sarah.

   – CER

ISBN-10: 1-58978-111-2
ISBN-13: 978-1-58978-111-5

WWW.ATLAS-GAMES.COM

THE ANTARCTIC EXPRESS

On September 2, many years ago, I lay in my bed. It would not have mattered if I had rustled my sheets, or how loudly I breathed. The Boston subway would rattle and roar, through dark tunnels under my house, running between stations even at midnight.

"You can't hear the subway all the way upstairs," my sister had insisted, but I knew she was wrong.

Late that night I did hear sounds, though not of hissing steam or squeaking metal. From outside came the sounds of whirring propellers and rumbling engines. I looked through my window and saw an airplane standing perfectly still in front of my house.

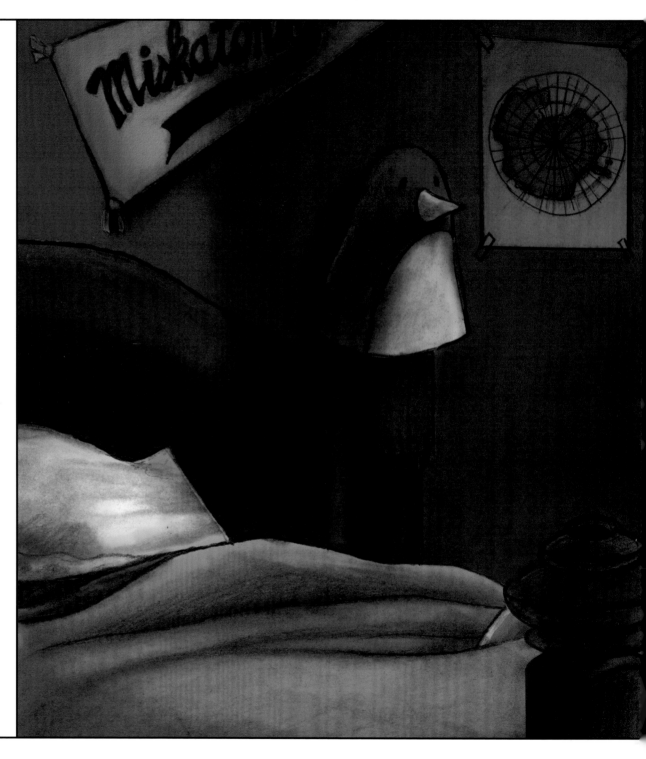

It was wrapped in an apron of fog. Snowflakes fell lightly around it. Professor Dyer stood at the open door of the plane. He took a sheaf of notes from his tweed coat, then looked up at my window. I put on my boots and jacket. I tiptoed downstairs and out the door.

"Now boarding," the professor said. I ran up to him.

"Well," he said, "are you coming?"

"Where?" I asked.

"Why, beyond the South Pole of course," was his answer. "This is the Antarctic Express." I took his outstretched hand and he pulled me aboard.

The plane was filled with other students, all in their coats and parkas. We talked about geology and Poe, and ate canned beef and hardtack. We drank cold lime juice, tasting sweet and sour all at once. Outside, the lights of cities and ships flickered below us as the Antarctic Express raced southward.

Soon there were no more lights to be seen. We traveled over frozen seas, where white-bellied penguins gazed up at our plane as it thundered over the empty wilderness.

We flew toward mountains so high it seemed as if they would scrape the moon. But the Antarctic Express never slowed down. Faster and faster we flew along, skimming over peaks and through valleys like a car on a roller coaster.

The mountains climbed higher, and became snow-covered plains. We crossed a barren desert of ice — the Great Plateau of Leng. Shapes appeared in the distance. They looked like gigantic cubes and tumbled blocks. "There," said the professor, "we are beyond the South Pole."

It was a huge city standing alone at the bottom of the world, filled with cones and bridges and dark tunnel mouths.

At first we saw no movement.

"Head for the center of the city," the professor said. "That is where Lake was investigating his specimens."

"Who gets to study with Lake?" we all asked.

The professor answered, "He will choose one of you."

"Look," shouted one of the students, "it is Lake's camp." Outside we saw torn tents and smashed sleds, but no people and no specimens. As our plane dropped closer to the center of the city, we slowed to a crawl, so carefully did we look for Lake. When the Antarctic Express could fly no slower, we landed and the professor led us outside.

We looked through the tents and came to the edge of a large, open circle. In front of us stood one of the sleds. The dogs were excited. They pranced and paced, jingling their collars and harnesses. Above their noise I could hear a strange sound. It was a high, whistling cry, like nothing I'd ever heard. Across the circle, the professor dug in the snow. An Old One was buried there. The students watched curiously.

The professor marched over to us and, pointing to me, said, "Come see this specimen here." I looked at the Old One and wondered where it had come from, and why it was buried standing up. I wondered whether Lake had found other Old One bodies, and where they had gone.

The professor handed me onto the sled. I sat on the bench and he asked, "Now, what would you like to learn here?"

I knew that I could learn any thing I could imagine from Professor Dyer. But the things I wanted to learn most were not outside, but deep in the city of the Old Ones. When I asked, the professor smiled. Then he gave me a hug and told a student to hook up the sled's harness.

We went into the biggest building, and began to follow the hallways deeper into the city. On the walls, we saw pictures of the Old Ones with palm trees and dinosaurs, ordering bubbling black blobs to build their city. The professor stood, holding a lantern high above him, and called out, "The first life on Earth!"

The professor read that the blobs were called shoggoths, and they had grown tired of building things for the Old Ones. They tried to pull off the Old Ones' heads, and so the Old Ones had run away into a hidden ocean inside the city.

We just had to find that ocean, even if we had to leave the sled here. We followed the carvings down a long tunnel and onto a ramp. At the bottom of the ramp, giant white penguins surprised us.

Below them lay the missing Old Ones!

They were not frozen any more, but their heads were gone.

Then we heard a strange sound from deep below us, a high, whistling cry of "Tekeli-li!" We ran back up the ramp as fast as we could. The piping shriek kept coming, "Tekeli-li! Tekeli-li!" We looked back once and saw a bubbling black blob — a shoggoth! It filled the whole tunnel from floor to ceiling and poured up toward us.

At the top of the tunnel we found our sled. Professor Dyer shouted out the dogs' names and cracked his whip. The dogs charged forward and pulled us back to the plane. The professor helped me down from the sled, and we climbed aboard.

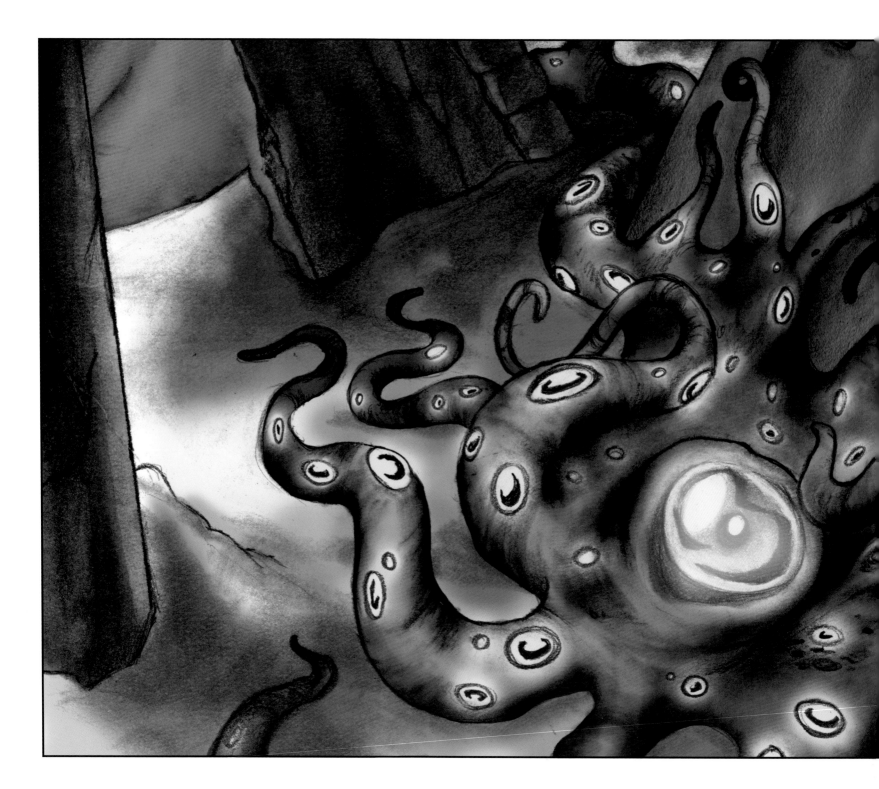

As soon as we were back inside the Antarctic Express, the other students wanted to know what happened, and what was making that shrill cry. I tried to explain, but my mind was blank. I had forgotten every thing of the Old One city. "Let's hurry outside and look ourselves," one of the students said. But the plane gave a sudden lurch and started moving. The Antarctic Express let out a roar from its propellers and sped away into the cold, dark polar sky. We were on our way home.

On Christmas Eve, my sister and I were shopping for presents. We decided to ride the subway back to our house. Down on the platform, we could both hear the Boston subway rattle and roar through the tunnels. Then it blew its whistle in a piping shriek; a whistling cry that I remembered all at once!

I dropped my packages and ran up the steps.

My sister had not heard any strange sound.

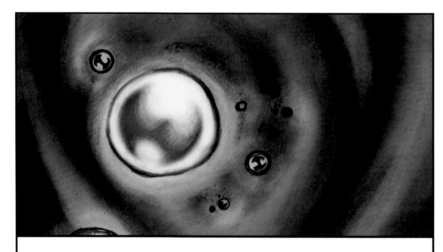

At one time everyone on the expedition had heard the whistling cry, but as years passed, it fell silent for all of them, or so they claimed. Even Professor Dyer insisted that he could no longer hear the piping shriek. Though I've grown old, the cry still echoes for me as it truly must for all who ever hear it: "Tekeli-li!"